Gorillas Go Bananas

Written by **Patrick Wensink**

Illustrated by **Nate Wragg**

HARPER

An Imprint of HarperCollinsPublishers

NO BANANAS WERE HARMED IN THE MAKING OF THIS BOOK.

To Kirsten and Nancy.
Thanks for making this dream come true.
—P.W.

For my mom. Thank you for not going bananas
when I was a picky little monkey.
—N.W.

Look up and you'll see 'em, high in the trees . . .

Bright yellow bunches in ones, twos, and threes.

Bananas! Bananas!

The jungle's insane.

A delicious delight on every ape's brain.

"Baby," says Mama, "come here, wash your feet.
Daddy is home, and he's brought you a treat!"

Then in swings his papa.
He carries a plate.

Now Baby thinks, "Wow! This treat will be great!"

"This sandwich is called the Elvis A. Presley. The chef who created it? Great-Uncle Leslie!

Like a PB and J, but we grill up the bread,

and no jelly for us. It's bananas instead!"

That little gorilla pops out a pink tongue.
He seems pretty picky for someone so young.
But these apes have big plans for feeding their child.
"This meal is too boring. He needs something wild!"

Minutes soon vanish and recipes fly. . . .
Tons of new dishes for Baby to try.

Piping-hot treats that smell quite tremendous,
top secret meals that taste simply stupendous.

Dad brings a bowl of bananas au gratin . . .
But Baby refuses. His face has gone rotten.
Banana chips served with green guacamole.
Stacks upon stacks of plantain ravioli.

They slice and they dice up their whole inventory,

fixing a batch of
bananas tandoori!

A gentle soufflé with a flaming flambé?

Banana-roll sushi?
A side of tempeh?

Baby won't eat. Mom and Dad start to worry.

He turns down a bowl of banana Thai curry.

Of course! Mama now knows why Baby won't eat.
These meals are too savory when they should be sweet.

Bananas get cooked every which way but loose:
Pancakes and strudel and squeezed into juice!

A seventeen-layer banana Bundt cake?
Enough 'nana smoothies to fill up a lake?

But Baby sits silent. His mouth does not budge.
He growls at the sight of banana-nut fudge

"I surrender,"

they say, and collapse onto the ground,
where a spent pile of peels
is all to be found.

The kitchen is wrecked thanks to all of their stunts—
and they still have no clue what it is Baby wants!
They've used every ingredient under the sun.
And every banana! Except for just one.

Baby scoots over. He peels and he eats.

He devours the treat with his hands and his feet.

But a plain old banana is all Baby wanted?"

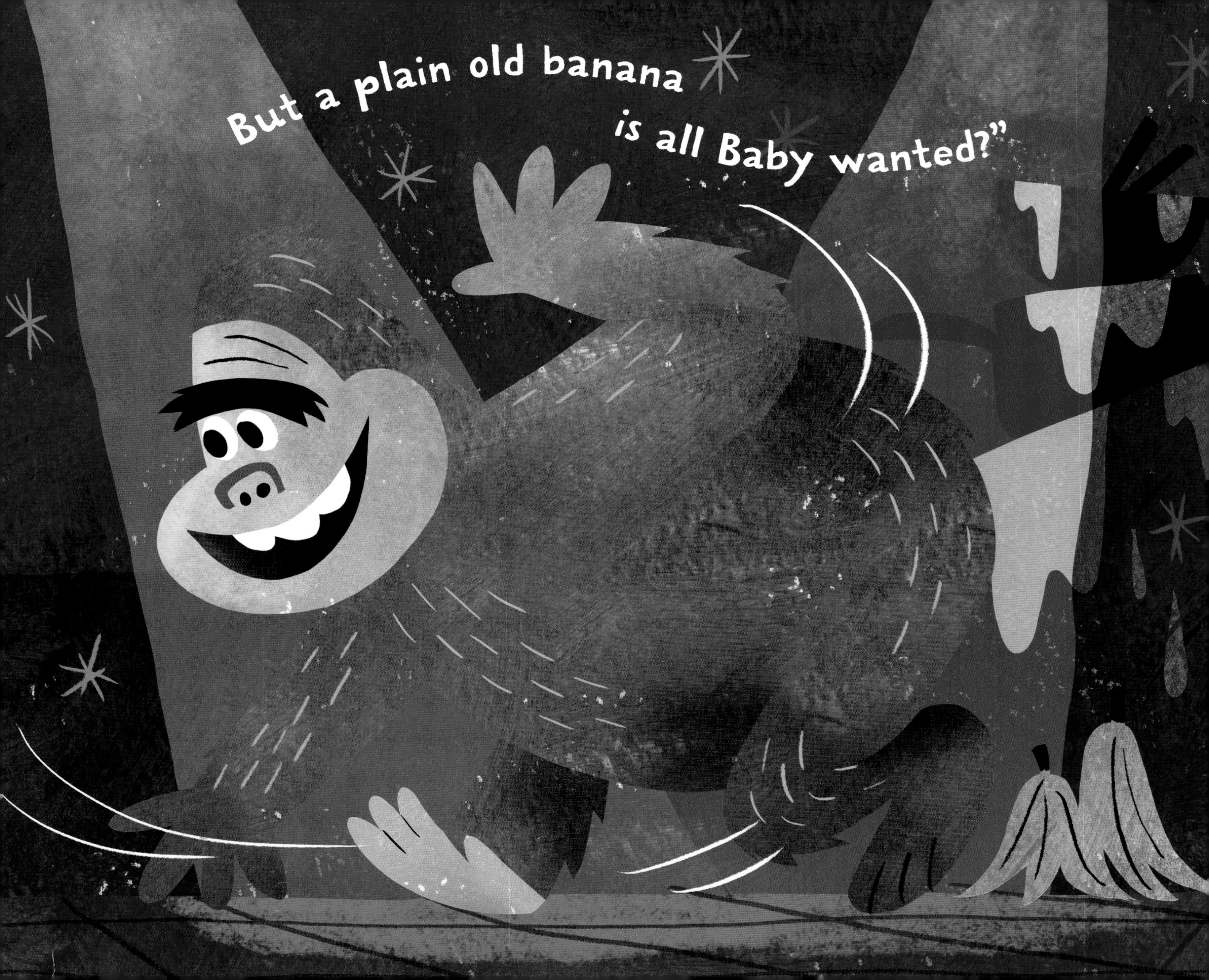